THE SKIRT CHASER

A LOVER

BHARGAVA REDDY CHINTHAREDDY

"I would like to dedicate this book to the Indian Army, Navy and air force who fight for the mother nation of India.

I would also like to dedicate this book to the army of all countries that try to protect their mother countries.

I would also dedicate this book to the people who flirt with others and are true lovers."

Contents

Preface

How a businessman loves and gets married. Once there was a good businessman goes by a business tycoon. He owns different types of businesses worth billions of money. He mostly never attended any meetings and his personal assistant will take care of most of the company affairs and sends every report to him by evening. He attends only the important meetings and others that he never attended any event or anything. Most of the employees and contractors don't even know how he looks only the board members know him.

Acknowledgements

I here hereby pledge that my work is genuine and isn't copied from any other sources. Everything in this book is fictional and is not based on anyone's life.

Prologue

How a businessman loves and gets married. Once there was a good businessman goes by a business tycoon. He owns different types of businesses worth billions of money. He mostly never attended any meetings and his personal assistant will take care of most of the company affairs and sends every report to him by evening. He attends only the important meetings and others that he never attended any event or anything. Most of the employees and contractors don't even know how he looks only the board members know him.

Introduction

Once there was a good businessman goes by a business tycoon. He owns different types of business companies in the name of Astar which is worth around billions of money and all located in the Astar companies line. Which is an industrial area and shopping area. He mostly never attended any meetings and his personal assistant will take care of most of the company affairs and sends every report to him by evening. He attends only the important meetings and other than that he never attended any event or anything. Most of the employees and contractors don't even know how he looks only the board members know him. He never gives any interviews to any channel or newspaper.

Most of the time he chases girls and flirts with them and he never crosses his line even if they tempt him. Most of the time his father James take care of the business and let him be like he was. He always flirts with girls by doing various jobs for fun and to understand people. One day he met a girl and get married at the age of 27 and take over the company's responsibilities as the head.

Introduction Of Character's

Albert - Main character, Business tycoon

James - Albert's father

Alfred - Albert's Best Friend, Albert's personnel assistant

Jasmine - Albert's first love

Rebecca - Albert's second love, interested in the status and luxury

Catherine - Albert's third lover, assistant lecturer, interested in money and luxury

Marie - Albert's wife, Albert's fourth lover

Jackson - Marie's father

Danya - Alfred's lover and wife

Edward - Albert's business rival

Michael - Alfred and Danya's son

Daniel - Albert and Marie's son

Julie - Albert and Marie's daughter

1

Schooling

Albert lost her mother at an early age and never get close to anyone of his age. Due to that, he has no friends and he never trusts anyone other than his father because one of his father's friend killed his mother. From that day onwards he stopped trusting others and don't like to make friends with anyone. The day before Albert went to join the school he asked his father to hide his identity in school to not get any high attention in school and his father agreed with him. On the day of school, James asked Albert why he wants to hide his identity in school then Albert replied that he wants to make friends who like him by his nature but not by money or others.

On the first day of school Albert never talked with anyone at all and as the teacher asked everyone to introduce themselves Albert introduced himself and didn't say he is a rich kid or anything. He mentioned that his father was a worker in Astar companies. After school James went to school to pick up Albert from school in the evening. On their way home James asked Albert how was the school and Albert said that it was ok. On the same day night, Albert asked James that he don't want him to come to school to for dropping and pick up him at school then James asked why?. Albert said that he was coming in a grand car and people will know that he is a rich kid then James asked Albert how will he come and go to school then. Then Albert said that he will stay in the hostel and come home every weekend or when he would like to. James agreed to Albert and asked the principal for a special exception for Albert to leave the hostel as he likes and the principal agreed to James on one condition that Albert has to report to him when he is going to leave the hostel. James agreed to the principal condition and after a week Albert went to the hostel.

2

Hostel life

Albert joined the hostel and the principal allotted him a 2 members room for him. The other person is of the same age and is in his class Alfred. Alfred was a good person and always tries to make friends with Albert but Albert never mingle with him. After a few days, Albert slowly made friends with Alfred and they play with each other. They won't go to school or canteen or anywhere if one isn't there. On every weekend both of them go to their homes and Alfred brought some snacks from home sometimes and shares them with Albert.

Alfred helps Albert with his studies in the hostel room in the evening every day as Albert was not interested in studies. After studying for a few years in the same school Albert and Alfred become best friends. They help each other out in trouble moments. All the time when they're together Albert never takes Alfred to his home even once but Alfred takes Albert to his home sometimes whenever he likes. As Alfred's mother was a good chef in a hotel Albert likes her cooking and asks Albert to get some food for him. Whenever Albert likes to eat something special he takes Alfred to Alfred home along with him.

Sometimes when Alfred's mother was away for work Alfred cooks and Albert helps him with vegetables and ingredients. When Alfred cooks Albert eats sometimes without comments and sometimes with comments. Sometimes Albert tries cooking and most of the time it's a failure. Albert forces Alfred to eat the food he cooked and Alfred tries to escape from there.

After school, both of them joined the same college and the business education department. They both took a flat nearby the college and Alfred prepares the food for both of them. Albert skips most of the classes and flirts with the girls in the college or goes to the canteen. In the evening Alfred teaches and explains the classes of that day. Albert flirts with every girl he sees even when he went for grocery shopping in the nearby mart. Albert learn music, boxing and soccer when he was in school and Alfred learn music, karate and soccer when he was in school. Both of them are actively involved in games and college functions whenever they were announced by the college committee.

Albert and Alfred both started learning car driving in their final year of their education in college. Alfred prepared for the university entry entrance exam while Albert was continuing flirting with the girls and was never interested in the university entrance exam. Sometimes Alfred scolds Albert for neglecting his studies then Albert neglect Alfred and says that he wasn't interested in getting on into the university for higher education. After a few days, both of them attended the University entry exam and

Albert went on flirting with the girls that were attending the exam. Alfred takes him away from flirting with the girls and both of them had the exam.

4

University

After a few days, the results of the University entrance exam are released and Alfred got admitted to the university. While Albert wasn't interested in the university he went to some college for his master's in business. Alfred also went to university for his master's in business like Albert and both of them held a party on their last day in college.

After getting into the university Albert and Alfred contact each other on weekends and whenever Albert likes to meet Alfred, he went to him without any thinking. After a few months of getting into the university Alfred's mother died due to an accident in the restaurant and as soon as Alfred get the news of the accident he informed Albert. Both of them went to the hospital and performed the death ceremony for Alfred's mother and built a cemetery for her. After that Albert helped Alfred to get better from that situation and Albert stayed with Alfred for a few days. Albert left him in the university and went back to college.

After a few days, the University is going to ends and Alfred gets a letter from the Astar group of companies stating that he was selected for a job in their company. But in the letter, it doesn't state what kind of job it was so Alfred was confused. Along with the letter, there was a black card with a golden star on it and the letter stated that the card is necessary for entering the interview venue. Alfred explained everything about the letter to Albert and Albert said that it is a good opportunity for him to attend the interview. After the completion of university, Alfred went to the address mentioned in the letter.

5

Interview

Alfred along with Albert went to the Astar industrial area. After both of them entered the industrial area Albert left Alfred alone and said that he was going shopping by chasing after a girl to flirt with. After Albert went away Alfred went to the Astar company and showed the letter to the security. After the security saw the letter they directed Alfred to the central reception without asking any questions or anything. After reaching the reception, the receptionist asked for the letter and Alfred handed the letter to the receptionist. After seeing the letter the receptionist asked for is there any card with this letter then Alfred showed the black card with one star. After seeing that card the receptionist asked Alfred to have a seat for a few minutes and called James's assistant and explained everything to him. After a few minutes James assistant himself to Alfred and take Alfred to James's cabin directly for an interview.

After entering the James cabin Alfred greeted James with respect and benevolence and James greeted Alfred in return. After greeting each other Alfred had a seat and James interviewed for about an hour. After the completion of the interview, James asked Albert to wait at the reception for his appointment letter. After that Alfred went to the reception hall and waited there. After a few minutes, James came to Alfred and asked him to come with him to his home for lunch, Alfred went with James after informing Albert that he is going to have lunch with James.

Both of them went to James's house and James asked Alfred to have a seat. After that James called his butler and ordered him to get some tea for 3 people. After the butler left, Alfred asked why did he order to bring tea for 3 people then James asked Alfred to see the appointment letter.

Alfred saw the letter and in the letter, it was written that he is responsible for being a personal assistant to his son. After reading the letter, Alfred asked James who is the person he was going to work for and in the meantime, the butler brought the tea. James asked the butler to call Romeo here and the butler went upstairs. After a few minutes, Albert came down from upstairs and Alfred was shocked on seeing Albert. James asked Alfred why he was shocked, and then Alfred asked is he your son sir. James said that Albert is his son and Alfred's friend. After that Albert explained everything to Alfred and said his name was Albert Romeo.

♡♡♡

6

Albert and Alfred

After having lunch Albert takes Alfred to a small village near the town which is almost near to the forest and explained everything about why Albert hides his identity as a rich person. Alfred understand Albert's reason and said to leave it be. After the discussion, both of them enjoyed themselves a lot by making food and making jokes against each other. While both of them enjoying James came alone and joined them and by late-night Albert went to sleep.

After Albert went to his room James thanked Alfred and Alfred asked James why are you thanking me, sir?. James replied to Alfred's question by giving a smile "for taking care of him all along till now" and "Alfred replied that Albert was his friend and he was responsible for him". Then James said, Alfred, it's not an easy task to take care of Albert and Albert became happier after meeting with you in the school. He tells me everything about you when he comes back home on weekends or holidays and James said some other things about Albert.

After James completed telling Albert's story to Alfred, Alfred asked James in a low voice "sir did Albert ever mention about flirting with girls?". Then James said that

Alfred just call me uncle and said that Albert never mentioned such things to me. James asked Alfred that does Albert flirts with girls?. And Alfred is going to say yes Albert suddenly came and closed Alfred's mouth. After seeing Albert, Alfred went silent and Albert dragged Alfred to his room and asked him to don't tell him anything about flirting with girls to his father and Alfred agreed to him without asking anything. After that for a few days, both of them stayed there and Albert explained everything about his businesses. Before the day of Alfred's joining day, Albert promised his father and Alfred that they have to take care of the business until he turns 27 and gets married. After promising them he left in the morning without telling anything to them. On the day of Alfred's joining day, James announced that Alfred will be the acting director in his absence.

7

Jasmine

After leaving the village Albert went to a small shop for a part-time job. He works as a cashier in the shop and flirts with young girls who come for shopping while billing. One day Albert met Jasmine in the shop and flirted with her and she got mad at him. After a week, Jasmine came shopping again and Albert flirted with her. Jasmine got irritated and Albert asked her to cool down. After a few words from Albert, Jasmine cooled down a bit and Albert make friends with her. Later for a few days, Jasmine didn't come for shopping.

One day Jasmine came shopping and Albert started flirting with her then she stopped Albert. After stooping Albert, Jasmine asked Albert why he flirts with every girl and Albert said that he was happy and made people around him happy by flirting with them. Albert said to Jasmine, that flirting is not commenting on one but making them feel better by saying some beautiful words. After what Albert said, Jasmine gave her number to Albert and asked for his number then Albert gave his number to her.

On the same day evening, Jasmine made a call to Albert and talked for about an hour to make her friendship with

Albert better. Time flies like the wind and a few days passed away before knowing and Alfred got the news of Albert. One day Alfred met Albert and warned him "if he didn't contact him regularly, he will resign from his position and never contact you anymore." with a serious tone. Albert agreed to Alfred's condition and on that day evening, Albert introduced Jasmine to Alfred. After that, all of them had dinner at a hotel and Albert went to send off Jasmine to her home. After Jasmine left Alfred asked Albert did he told her about his identity and Albert replied that he didn't tell her yet. After that, they discussed some business matters and Alfred left.

After a few days, Albert fell in love with Jasmine and Jasmine also fall in love with Albert. Albert proposed to Jasmine one day and she accepted his love proposal. After a few days of getting to know each other, one day Albert invited Jasmine for dinner and Jasmine accepted. On the same day evening, both of them went to a top hotel for dinner. After entering the hotel Albert takes Jasmine to the top floor for dinner. After that, both of them take a table and Albert ordered some food and wine. After that Albert recited a poem for her while the food will get ready and expressed it to her.

> “*"The dark sunset is beautiful,*
> *The light sunrise is wonderful,*
> *The valleys are sorrowful,*
> *The mountains are joyful,*
> *The world is colourful,*
> *The society is commandant,*
> *The love is hateful,*
> *The hate of mine is for you."*”

After hearing that Jasmine said that was a good one and asked about the last two stanzas. Then Albert said the last two stanzas are from our second meeting where you and I are met with a small hatred that becomes love. In the two stanzas love comes from hate and hate is within love. As soon as Albert finished his words the waiter bring the dishes they ordered and they started dining after the dishes were served.

After finishing the dinner Albert said to Jasmine that he was the inheritor of Astar companies. Jasmine didn't believe Albert and she said stop kidding. Albert said that he wasn't kidding and Jasmine didn't believe Albert's words. Albert said the same thing in an angry voice and Jasmine said cool Albert. After Albert cooled down she said that she has a friend in the Astar company and her position is also high, so I will ask her about the inheritor of the Astar company. Albert agreed with Jasmine and asked Jasmine about her friend's name. After that Albert opened the Astar company website and Jasmine called her friend. After Albert opened the company website asked for Jasmine's friend's details and entered them into the website.

After a minute, Albert told every detail of her friend's data in the company profile including salary and employee unique number. Jasmine asked her friend the details that Albert told her and her friend asked her how did she know all that data about her. Then Jasmine told that one of her friends told her that and her friend asked for that person's name. Then Jasmine asked why and her friend said that only the director level person can only see the details of her in all over the Astar companies and Jasmine asked her friend "are you sure about it" in a shocked voice. Her friend said that she was sure about this then Jasmine asked have you ever seen your director's son. Then her friend said no and most of the employees even don't know his name and Jasmine asked her friend does she know his name. Then her friend said that she heard once his name was Albert Romeo and our current acting director Alfred was his only friend.

After hearing that Jasmine cut off the phone and was in shock. Then Albert said to Jasmine the same that her friend told her and made a break up with her and left the hotel after paying the bill. Before Albert left the hotel Jasmine asked Albert why did he break up with her then Albert said if she can't trust him in serious situations what is the meaning of love and left. The next morning Jasmine went to Albert's part-time work store with a gift to say sorry to him but she didn't find him there and she came there every day for about a week and can't find him. After that week she never came to that store again.

8

Rebecca

After breaking up with Jasmine, Albert quit his job and joined a taxi driver. As a taxi driver, he greets every customer who picks up his taxi for a ride and in some cases, he flirts with young girls. Sometimes he plays jokes with his customers to change their mood and most of the people who choose his taxi like him. On a busy day, Rebecca picked up Albert's taxi for a ride to an auction house and as Rebecca was tense, Albert tried to cool her by flirting but she got angered. Then Albert stayed quiet all the way to the auction house and after Rebecca got down and paying the money Albert asked Rebecca do girls have a hobby of misunderstanding words. After listening to those words Rebecca asked what are you saying then Albert said nothing, leave it and left by saying all the best for the auction.

One day Rebecca's father picked up Albert's taxi for a ride to the hospital for a health check and on the way Albert talked a lot with Rebecca's father. After reaching the hospital Rebecca's father asked him to stay for a while until he come back then Albert asked him "can I come with you" then Rebecca's father to said to come. Albert went with him to the hospital and after the checkup, Albert take him to his house for dropping. After reaching Rebecca's house Rebecca's father invited Albert for a cup of coffee and Albert went in along with Rebecca's father. After entering Rebecca's house Rebecca's father called Rebecca and asked her to prepare coffee. After a few minutes, Rebecca brought the coffee and saw Albert.

After seeing Albert she asked her father "what is he doing here?" with an angry voice and Rebecca's father explained everything. After hearing everything Rebecca asked about the words that Albert said to her at the auction house and Albert said that my previous girlfriend also has a good way of misunderstanding. So I think most of the girls have a great time misunderstanding the words of boys. So I said that sentence and Rebecca's father said that "Albert, you got a good knowledge of girls" with a smiling voice. Rebecca gets angered and Albert changed the topic immediately after seeing that Rebecca is getting angered. After that, they talked about some things and Albert said goodbye and left. Rebecca went to send off Albert and Rebecca thanked Albert. Albert asked Rebecca why did she thank him then Rebecca said making her father happy and Albert said that's OK. Albert said to Rebecca that flirting is changing people's moods and not in a wrong way in my thoughts and left.

A few days over and in that few days Albert and Rebecca met each other several times. Both of them are in love with each other and both of them are waiting for a situation to propose to other. One day Rebecca booked Albert's taxi and on the way to Rebecca's destination, Albert got a call from Alfred and picked up Alfred due to some business affairs. After picking up Alfred, Rebecca asked "who is he?" then Alfred introduced himself as Alfred and he was the personal assistant of the managing director of Astar companies. After a few minutes, Alfred asked Albert to sign some documents and after Albert signed the documents Alfred said bye and left the car. After Alfred left Rebecca asked Albert "who are you and what are the documents?". Albert invited Rebecca for dinner and that he will explain everything to her after dinner tomorrow. The next day evening, Albert went to Rebecca's house in a high-end car and take her to dinner in a hotel. Both of them went into the hotel and ordered some food and beverages. Albert said that he recited a poem for Rebecca and Rebecca asked him to tell her. Then Albert gave her a paper having a poem

> “*"The light that guides you,*
> *The dark that follows you,*
> *The time flows for you,*
> *The future looks for you,*
> *Good and bad are nothing,*
> *Ups and downs are everything,*
> *My life and love are for you,*
> *End of you always comes with mine."*”

After reading the poem Rebecca proposed to Albert with love and Albert also proposed to her. After that Rebecca asked about Albert's identity and as Albert is going to say the waiter came with the dishes they ordered.

Both of them completed the dishes and Albert said that he was the inheritor of the Astar companies. Rebecca was shocked and Albert said, that Alfred whom she met last day was his only friend. After that, she asked Albert why is he hiding his identity and then Albert said that he want a free and none restricted life. Rebecca understands everything that Albert said and after a few words of discussion both of them left the hotel after paying the bill. After that a few days went by in a blink of an eye, one day Rebecca asked Albert to take over his position as managing director of the company and said that she want to introduce him to her friends as managing director of the Astar companies. Then Albert asked Rebecca why don't you introduce me as a taxi driver and then she said why do I have to do introduce him as a taxi driver when you're a rich man. Then Albert asked her if she was interested in prestige and status and she said yes. Then Albert made a breakup with her and left that place. After that incident, Albert changed his job and place. Later Rebecca called his phone and it didn't connect, Rebecca went to Astar companies to meet Alfred. Rebecca met Alfred and asked about Albert then he said that he don't know where Albert went and said that when he isn't in a good mood he will go somewhere without contacting anyone until he gets a mood change. After hearing all that Rebecca left and tried to call Albert.

9

Catherine

After their breakup with Rebecca Albert joined as a junior lecturer in a small college. In the college, Albert met Catherine who is a junior lecturer like him in the same college and both of them are in the same department. Albert oftenly flirts with Catherine who is a campus beauty and he also flirts with some female students in the classes he attends one day every week. Sometimes he flirts with students after the classes and outside the college on weekends. Albert enjoyed life in the college as a junior lecturer a lot and holds up a party whenever he likes and invites his students to the party.

A few days passed and Albert and Catherine became good friends. Sometimes Catherine also attends Albert's party and stays there all that night and attends goes to her home in the morning. After a few days, Catherine fell in love with Albert but she never expressed it to him and didn't say anything to anyone about her love for Albert. After a few days, Albert also fell in love with Catherine and he didn't express it to her. One day Catherine went to Astar companies due to some work there and Albert also went there due to some board of directors meeting that he has to attend the meeting.

After the meeting and Albert exiting the company with Alfred, Catherine saw Albert and Catherine didn't meet Albert and left the Astar companies. On the weekend Catherine invited Albert for lunch at her home and Albert agreed to go to her home for lunch on weekend. The weekend has arrived and Albert went to Catherine's home for lunch. Catherine introduced her family members to Albert and Catherine and her mother went into the kitchen to prepare lunch. In the meantime, Albert and Catherine's father discussed some business and marketing ideas. After a few minutes, Catherine came and said that lunch is ready and dragged Albert to the dining table because Albert and Catherine's father were continuing their discussion after hearing Catherine's words.

After a while, they started eating their lunch and after lunch, Catherine asked Albert what is he doing at Astar companies on that day and Albert said that he will explain everything to her on another day and left Catherine's house. After a week, in the morning Albert called Catherine on the phone and invited Catherine for lunch and said that he will pick her up in the afternoon. In the afternoon Albert went to Catherine's house and picked up her in a luxurious car. On the way, Catherine asked Albert where did he get such a luxurious car and Albert said that she will know in a while. After a while, Albert takes Catherine to a big home and Catherine asked Albert "this isn't your home" and Albert said this isn't his house, but his best friend's home. After entering the house Albert shouted "Alfred" and Alfred come out of his room and asked why is he shouting like that.

Albert said to take it easy man and introduced Catherine to Alfred and Alfred to Catherine. After introducing each other Albert asked Alfred to prepare lunch and Alfred asked

Albert and Catherine to cut the vegetables and prepare spices for cooking. Both of them started chopping vegetables and Alfred started cooking. After a few minutes, Alfred finished the dishes and all of them started lunch, during lunch Albert said that Alfred was the personal assistant of Astar companies managing director and acting managing director of Astar companies in the absence of the managing director. After that Albert said that day when Catherine saw Albert at Astar companies he went to meet Alfred and Alfred said the same to Catherine. After lunch, all of them had a chat for about an hour and Catherine and Albert left after saying bye to Alfred. On the way back to Catherine's home Albert gave a small piece of paper to Catherine and asked Catherine to open it after she reached her home and Albert dropped Catherine at her home and left after saying bye. After that Catherine went to her room and opened the paper that Albert gave and on that paper, a poem was written. Catherine read that poem.

“*"The fields are green,*
With yellow paint from the sun,
The snow is white,
With the light from the moon,
The oceans are blue,
With the reflection of the sky,
The life is full of love,
With the tears of the heart."”

After reading the poem Catherine called Albert and proposed her love to him and Albert also proposed to her. After proposing Catherine asked Albert about the meaning of the last line of the poem and Albert said that he will later and ended the call. After that, a few days passed, one day

Catherine asked Albert how did he know Alfred and Albert said both of them are childhood friends. Then Catherine asked Albert to ask Alfred for a job in Astar companies for him and Albert asked Catherine "why?". Then Catherine said that Astar companies are big business associations and the salary would be high and we can have a happy life. After hearing all that Albert said no to Catherine and said that he wants to do things as he wants and never wants to depend on anyone.

After that a few days passed, the college is going to end and on the last day of the Academic year, Albert hold a party at his home and invited Catherine to the party along with the students. Albert and all the others enjoyed the party a lot and except for Catherine, everyone left the party. After a few minutes, Albert said that he was the inheritor of Astar companies to Catherine and Catherine asked Albert why is he working as an assistant professor in such a small college. Then Albert said that he isn't interested in the business and wants to live a carefree life like now and Catherine said that "are you mad or what" in an angry voice. Then Albert asked Catherine if she was that interested in money and Catherine said yes and with that status and everything comes to oneself. After that, both of them went to sleep and the next day Albert went to college and resigned from his position in college. After that, Albert called Catherine on phone and said that he would like to break up with her. After that, he said that most of the people's lives are filled with tears and that is the meaning of the last 2 stanzas of the poem that he recited and that tears come from money and cut the call. After that, Catherine tried to call Albert but didn't connect and one day Catherine went to Alfred like Rebecca and Alfred said the same thing as he said to Rebecca.

10

Marie

After the breakup with Catherine, Albert went to a small town near the sea shoreline without doing any job and enjoying life. Like that, a few days passed and one-day Albert went to the bank to withdraw money from his account and saw his college principal Jackson in the bank. Albert greeted his principal with a gentle voice and Jackson also greeted Albert with a gentle voice. After that Jackson asked Albert about his career and Albert said that he is planning to do a business in this area. After hearing that Jackson asked Albert "are you interested in doing a partnership business" in a normal voice with some tension on his face and Albert agreed to that. After that Albert asked Jackson why did he come to the bank and Jackson said that he retired from the college and come to the bank for applying for a loan.

After that Albert and Jackson left the bank and after a week Albert met Jackson and asked about the loan. Then Jackson said that the banks are asking for security or mortgage for issuing the loan and then Albert said that he will ask Alfred to sign up for security for the loan. After that Albert called Alfred and asked them to sign the document as a security for the loan for Jackson and the next day Alfred came to the bank and after reaching the bank Alfred greeted Jackson and Albert all of them entered the bank. Alfred signed the loan documents as security for the loan based on his job. After the completion of the bank documents, all of them went to Albert's house and hold a party and After the party, Jackson and Alfred left.

After a week, Jackson's loan got approved by the bank and Jackson went to Albert to discuss about the business partnership. After the discussion about the business partnership, Albert asked Jackson what type of business he wants to start. Then Jackson said his ideas to Albert and Albert choose a canteen on the beach and Jackson also agreed. After that, a few days passed and in that time Albert did all the legal work for establishing a canteen on the beach and Jackson did all the construction work along with Albert. Both of them named the canteen as "A & M food and beverages".

After a week, Marie came to the canteen instead of Jackson and Albert introduced himself to Marie. On the same day evening, Albert asked Marie why didn't Jackson come to the canteen today and Marie said that her father isn't feeling well so that she came to the canteen. After that Marie comes to the canteen frequently to the canteen instead of Jackson and Albert flirted with her and both of them fell in love with other but didn't propose to each other.

After a few days, Marie's birthday comes and Jackson holds a party to celebrate Marie's birthday. Jackson invited Albert and Alfred to Marie's birthday party and both of them attended the party, Albert introduced Alfred to Marie. After that, the party started and everyone enjoyed the party a lot. After the party, Albert proposed to Marie by giving her a letter and a gift as a birthday present and asked her to read it after entering her room. Later Marie went to her room and opened the letter after she get fresh up. In the letter, Albert proposed and write a poem for Marie.

“"The looks in your eyes
Is as beautiful as
The red clouds formed during
The sunset in the evening time,
The voice from your mouth
Is as beautiful as
The music that comes formed by
The humming of birds in the forest,
The glow in your face
Is as beautiful as
The dance of a tree caused by
The blowing winds that come from the sea,
The heart of yours
Is as vast as
The skies that that covered by
The white running clouds to its home,
The soul of yours is connected to mine
As soon as it comes from the heavens
To fill the world with glow as brighter as
the glow of the moonlight in the sky at night."”

After reading the letter Marie called Albert on phone and proposed to him. After that, both of them talked a lot and went to bed by midnight. Jackson didn’t know that Marie and Albert are in love with each other and like that a few days passed. Both of them, roam on the beach everyday evening after closing the canteen. One day Jackson gets to know that Albert and Marie are in love with each other and asked Marie about their love. Marie said, yes to Jackson and

Jackson didn't accept her love. Marie called Albert on the phone and said that her father didn't accept their love.

The next day morning, Albert went to Jackson's house with documents in his hand and handed the documents to Jackson after entering the house. After that Albert called Marie and Marie came and both of them left Jackson's house. After they both went out, Jackson read the documents and in that documents that his shares in the canteen have transferred to Jackson. After reading the documents Jackson called Albert on the phone and Marie picked up the phone. Jackson asked Marie to hand over the phone to Albert then Marie said that they are going to get married soon and handed over the phone to Albert. After Albert takes the phone, Jackson asked why did he transfer all his shares to Jackson. Then Albert said, that he don't need that shares and cut the call.

After the call, Marie asked Albert the same thing that Jackson asked him and Albert said that he is the inheritor of Astar companies. After hearing that Marie asked Albert why is he hiding his identity and Albert said that he isn't interested in business and want to live a free life. Then Marie said that it was alright and Marie went to the kitchen to cook and Albert called Alfred on the phone and invited him for lunch at his home.

Alfred came to Albert's house for lunch with his lover Danya and after entering Alfred introduced Danya to Alfred and Marie. After that Alfred said that they were going to get married soon. After that all of them had lunch and after lunch, they had a small chat. After that Alfred and Danya left and Marie stay with Albert in Albert's house. After a few days, Alfred and Danya got married and Alfred hold a party for his wedding. After a few days, Albert reached 27 years and James held a big banquet for Albert's birthday party. At the birthday party, James announced Albert as the heir of Astar companies Albert Romeo and announced Albert's and Marie's wedding after a few days. After a few days, Albert and Marie got married.

ᑭᑭᑭ

11

Albert life

After a few days of Albert's marriage with Marie, one day Albert met Jasmine at a shopping mall and invited her to lunch in a restaurant. Jasmine went with Albert to a restaurant for having lunch and after entering the restaurant Jasmine asked Albert why did he break up with her, then Albert said that he will tell her that later. Later that they both ordered some dishes for lunch and Albert asked Jasmine how is she doing, then she said that she was doing alright and got married a few days ago. After that, the dishes that they ordered has been served and while eating Jasmine how was Albert doing, then Albert said that he had takeover the Astar companies and gotten married a few days ago like her. After the completion of the lunch, Albert said that she didn't trust him when he said that he was the inheritor of Astar companies and without trust, no love would exist and that is the reason he break up with her. After that, he paid the bill and left the restaurant by saying bye to Jasmine.

After a few days, Danya and Marie got pregnant almost at nearly the same time. One day Albert, Alfred, Marie and Danya went to a movie in the evening and after the movie, all of them went to a restaurant for dinner and they had their full and returned to Albert's house. On their way home, around 20 hooligans followed his car and Albert lead them to a secluded area. After entering the secluded area, Albert and Alfred get down from the car and locked the car. As soon as the hooligans saw Albert and Alfred, all of them also get down from their cars and prepared to attack both of them. Both Alfred and Albert beat all of the hooligans to the ground and handed them to the police for investigation.

After a week or so the police send their investigation report to Albert stating that one of the clients Edward whom he rejected sent the hooligans against him. In the late afternoon, both Albert and Alfred both went to Edward's office without an appointment and warned him if he ever tries to make enemies with them they will not leave him alone and left. The next day, Albert ordered Alfred to buy some shares of Edward's company and Alfred said that he did that already. After a few days, Danya give birth to a boy and Alfred named him Michael. After that, around 2 weeks passed and Marie give birth to a boy and Albert named him Daniel.

The next day Albert gifted a mansion to Marie in a small town near the forest. After that, Marie asked that she want to see Jackson and Albert agreed to her request. The next day Albert went to Jackson's house and get to know that he changed his house and sold the canteen on the beach. After that Albert handed over the business affairs and Marie's care to Alfred and left in search of Jackson.

After a few days of search, Albert found Jackson's whereabouts and went there for Jackson. Jackson went to that address and met Jackson. After that, he met Jackson and Jackson invited Albert inside and offered some coffee. After having a cup of coffee Albert explained everything to

Jackson and asked Jackson to visit Marie. Jackson went with Albert to see Marie and Marie felt very happy after seeing Jackson. That day Marie prepared a variety of dishes for Albert and Jackson.

12

Catherine death

After a few days, Albert met Catherine in a restaurant and Catherine came to Albert and greeted him. Albert greeted her back and asked about her well being. She said she was doing well and asked about Albert well being. Then Albert said that he was doing well as the director of Astar companies and had a son a few days ago. After that Catherine take Albert's contact number and left the restaurant after paying the bill.

After a few days, Catherine called Albert on phone and asked him to go for a ride and Albert rejected her. The next day Catherine called Albert on the phone and asked him for a ride again and Albert rejected her again. After a week, Albert gets a courier containing photos of Albert and Catherine along with a letter stating that if he didn't call her she will send the photos to the press. Then Albert called Catherine on the phone and told Catherine that he'll take her to a place after a week and asked her to be prepared. After saying that Albert cut the call with Catherine.

After a week, Albert went to pick Catherine up and take her to the mansion in the village that he own. After reaching the mansion Albert take Catherine into the mansion and asked the butler to get some coffee and snacks for both of them and went to his room along with Catherine. After entering the room Albert asked Catherine why is she bugging him like that and Catherine said that she want some ransom as he was the director of Astar companies. After hearing that Albert asked how much she want and Catherine said that half of his shares in Astar companies. After hearing that Albert was shocked for a sec and said that he need some time to get that done and Catherine agreed with Albert's words.

On that day late evening, Albert and Catherine had some alcohol after having some snacks and Albert said that she isn't going to live past this day to Catherine. After hearing that Catherine, she asked Albert that is he going to kill her and Albert said yes to Catherine's words. After hearing those words Catherine got shocked and asked Albert for his car keys. Albert gave the keys to Catherine and went to another room for rest. The next morning police officer came to Albert and informed him that Catherine met an accident last night and expired. Albert was shocked and asked the officer how the accident occurred and where it occurred. The officer said that the accident occurred last night and some eyewitnesses stated that she was driving crazily. After saying all that the officer asked Albert does anything wrong happened last day and Albert said that both of them had some alcohol last night. After that, the officer said that he will contact him later whenever necessary for the investigation and left.

ᚹᚹᚹ

13

Albert's and Marie's life

After a week of Catherine's death, the police officers closed the case as an accident and Albert went back home. After that a few days passed and Marie got pregnant. Michael and Daniel both started attending the same school and become good friends like Albert and Alfred. After that, a few months passed and Marie give birth to a baby girl and Albert named her Julie. Around 2 years later Jackson died due to an illness that he is having for a long time.

After Jackson's death, Marie is mentally disturbed, and Albert didn't go to the office for some time. In the meantime, Danya and Alfred also stayed at Albert's house at that time. After a few months, Marie gets better and Alfred and Danya get back to their own house. After that a few days passed and one day suddenly James got bedridden and the doctors said that he doesn't have much time to live. After that a few days passed away and James does and Alfred stayed with Albert for a few days to console him. After that a few days passed away, one-day income tax officers came to Astar companies and on that day Albert was n leave and Alfred was taking Albert's place and showed all the documents asked by the officers. The income tax raid went up to a week all around the Astar companies and its associated companies.

After that, a few years passed, Daniel and Edward, turned 25 and Albert handover the Astar companies to Daniel by holding a banquet for Daniel's 25th birthday. Albert assigned Edward as Daniel's personnel assistant like he had Alfred. because both Edward and Daniel are good friends like Albert and Alfred. After a few days, Edward and Julie get married as both of them are in love with each other and both Albert and Alfred agreed to their marriage. After a few months, Marie got sick and bedridden, in that few days Alfred and danya met an accident and both of them died. As the passing day, Marie's health got bad and one day Marie asked Albert to promise one thing and asked for the truth about Catherine's death.

Albert said that he will tell her and told her that he removed the brake wires of the car and appeared in front of Catherine's car that day near the accident spot and to avoid him Catherine diverted the car into the forest and the accident occurred. After that Marie asked Albert why he killed her and Albert said he killed her because she blackmailed him and said that if he give her what she asked, she will blackmail him again. After that said that's why he killed her. After that a few days passed away and Marie died due to her illness and the next day Albert committed suicide and expired.

ÞÞÞ

About The Author

"Bhargava Reddy Chinthareddy"

This is the second book that I have ever written and I think it's a great one. I don't know when I'll write the next one. I never say anything like I like to write books or anything because most people know that's a lie. so I will say that if you like my book please read the other books that I write in the future. I would like to thank you for reading my book. I had an accident in 2021 and in march 2022 I started writing the book for some earnings for myself to live. Failures aren't stepping stones to success but barriers that you have to overcome that's what I believe.

End Matter

This book is about love and what is love in my view. It may hurt some of your feeling and Iwould like to apology in beforehand if this book hurt any of your feeling. Finally, the conclusion of this book is love isn't based on money or status or luxury comes from them

Books By This Author

The Lost Blacksmith General

once there was an emperor in an empire that goes by the name Heavens land. Which consists of some small kingdoms. Their empire was very prosperous under the emperor's rule. The emperor never wages a war against any other empires even though he can win against them but if any empire wages war against his empire he will completely defeat them and make theirs under his ruling. The story of a mighty general who lost everything in his life and lives alone in wild in search of happiness till his last breath. Did the general have a happy ending or a sad ending?

Is the soldier survived

The story is about a soldier who is isolated from his troops while helping them to retreat from war. How the isolated soldier survived in the enemy territory for about 48 days. What did the isolated soldier do in that few days in the enemy territory and how did he help his country in the next war by sending the enemy territory data to his country. Later in the war how he reunited with his troops and helped the war.

Printed by Libri Plureos GmbH in Hamburg,
Germany